THE *Family* SECRET

The Santini Family #2

S.L. Sinclair

Table of Contents

Partners in Crime Book Services

Copyright © 2022 S.L. Sinclair

All rights reserved.

No part of this book may be reproduced or

transmitted in any form or by

any means without written permission of the

author.

ISBN: 979-8-9988203-1-1

Dedication

To you, who survived everything life threw at you just to get you to this moment, right here, reading these words.
I am glad you're still here.
I may not know you, but I'm proud of you.

Content Warning

Please skip this page if you do not want a warning.

This book is meant for readers above the age of 18 due to sexual content, dubious consent, non-consent, stalking, physical abuse, murder.
It also includes MM+ content and incest.
Read at your own discretion.

Also by S.L. Sinclair

Wife for Hire

Beyond Her Duties

The Family Firm

The Family Secret

The Family Fortune

Call Me Danger

Don't Get Me Twisted

Perfect Martinis

Unbiased

Acts of Contrition

Her Secret Master

Perfect Disaster

The Vampire Mistress

Lie To Me

Playlist

"Cypher Pt. 3: Killer" by BTS feat. Supreme Boi

"Bad Decisions" by Benny Blanco, BTS, and Snoop Dogg

"Cool For The Summer" by Demi Lovato

"Left and Right" by Charlie Puth feat. Jung Kook

"Soothe My Soul" by Depeche Mode

"Jonestown Tea" by OTEP

"Trivia: Love" by BTS

"Gender" by Jonathan Davis

"Save ME" by BTS

"We Lost the Summer" by TOMORROW X TOGETHER

"Venom" by BVNDIT

Chapter One

Sasha

"**A**RE YOU SURE you're not missing something?"

I do my best to hold back my sigh. "No, Mom. I assure you, I finished every course. It's all submitted electronically. If I was missing something, I wouldn't be graduating."

Mom turns to look at me, and for one of the first times ever, I see real pride in her eyes. Shit, that's incredible. Almost makes me misty-eyed.

"A four-year Masters in criminal law, and you did it in two. I hope you know I'll be bragging everywhere," she tells me.

"As you should," I reply, neatly folding my gown into a pink cloth tote bag. I set my yellow cap on top of it.

"Valedictorian!" Mom's practically crowing now, and I bask in it. She and I don't usually see eye-to-eye. Hell, sometimes we don't see eye-to-toenail we're so different.

But I don't blame her for bragging. She had me when she was barely eighteen, and from what I can glean out of the bits and pieces she let slip, she has no idea who my father even is. Moms like her to kids like me were supposed to be the lowest of the low. Instead, she's a bigshot at a cosmetics company, and I'm about to enter law school at age twenty.

Damn right we should be proud of ourselves and bragging!

"I want to be you when I grow up," my younger half sister, Maggie, says, looking wistfully at the yellow gown.

"Nah, you wanna be you," I reply, wondering when she grew up so much. She looks a lot like me, just darker skinned because Daddy — her real dad, my former step dad — is dark-complexioned. His family hails from Sicily. "And you're going to be the best you there is."

Shit, I really feel sentimental. I sound like Doctor Seuss.

Caleb, my youngest sibling at age twelve, is the odd one out. He wants to go into tech, not law like the rest of the family. But Daddy supports him, and honestly, he's already great at repairing my electronics, like the time I accidentally broke a piece of my charger off in my Switch.

I yawn. It's barely eight am and it's already been a long day. I still have to sit through graduation, give a speech, and go out to a celebratory dinner with the whole family. "Whole" being us four, Daddy, his brother Uncle Tony, and Nonno, my step grandfather. Nonno's name is Anthony, Uncle Tony was named after him, and Daddy is named after his grandfather. Daddy and Uncle Tony are fraternal twins, and they don't even look related.

Mom and Daddy don't exactly get along great, but everyone else does, so they just sort of avoid talking directly to each other as much as they can during a get-together. Once we get over the initial awkwardness, it's fine.

Me, however, for the last two years I've been avoiding being in the same room with Mom and the guys. My siblings are different. But I guess I can't avoid awkwardness forever. At least this will just be a few hours.

And hopefully I can convince Mom to let me not stay at her house like I've been the past week.

She thinks I lived at the dorms, and since I finished my coursework early, obviously that meant I could come back to her place for the week between then and graduation.

Kinda sorta deliberately didn't tell her I only stayed at my dorm for exams and cramming. I mean, it's hard to concentrate on studying when you live with three hot guys who want to fuck even more than you do. The dorms were a good solution when I needed to work.

Mom, however, has no idea I've been seeing them for the past two years. And if everything goes according to plan, she never will get an idea.

"Ready to go?" she asks.

"Yes, as long as we can get coffee on the way. I'll be dead by dinner if I don't have at least three shots of espresso in me immediately," I reply.

But sadly, I do not get my coffee. The street is blocked off. From the front seat of Mom's car, I can count three police cars, the medical examiner's van, and an ambulance.

"I'm gonna be that person if I'm not caffeinated," I grumble. "I'm texting Daddy to bring coffees."

"Don't do that," Mom nearly whines as she does a U-turn to get down a different street.

"Too late." I fire off the text, knowing he'll bring me whatever I ask.

Due to the turnaround, we wind up getting to the university later than we intended. Daddy is waiting for us outside the doors, a tray of coffee in one hand, the other stuffed in his pocket.

Despite being forty-two, Daddy is movie-star handsome with messy brown hair and eternal stubble that doesn't look messy or sloppy. I see a few people giving him a second glance as they walk by.

I jump out of the car and grab my tote before Mom even finishes parking to run and give him a hug. In the same movement, I grab my triple shot iced macchiato from the tray.

Daddy laughs. "Are you more excited to see me or the coffee?"

"It's a tie," I tell him, smirking around the straw.

He goes to say something but stops when Maggie and Caleb, his biological kids, rush and hug him.

"Gene," Mom greets.

"Gina," Daddy replies. "You must be ecstatic about Sasha."

It was the right thing to say; Mom practically puffs up like a bird.

"Where are Nonno and Uncle Tony?" I ask, already halfway done with my drink. "I want to say hi before I get changed."

"Inside. We are putting the finishing touches on your graduation present." Daddy gives me a wink.

"Oooh, I'm going to go spoil the surprise," I say, rushing past him and in the doors.

Daddy and Uncle Tony are twins, but they don't look alike. Daddy is more toned and lithe, whereas Uncle Tony is broader with long, wild blond hair and tattoos with green eyes. He looks more like Nonno. Nonno's hair has gone white, but he still has the look of Alan Rickman circa 2009, and shares Uncle Tony's green eyes.

They're both easy to spot, especially since they're talking to two of my classmates, Daniel and Diana Choi. They're twins as well; seems I know more than the average person.

Diana's shoulder-length hair is pink, and Daniel's choppy hair is a blue green color. They stand out like crayons in a world of pencils.

Diana runs and greets me with a whisper, "Holy shit, why is your family so hot?"

"Step-family," I correct. "And I know. It's a problem."

She giggles. "Even Daniel thinks so. How do you control yourself around them?"

"Who says I do?" I reply, arching my eyebrows.

She gives a little playful squeal. "Oh my God, you're awful!"

We walk back over and Uncle Tony wraps me in a warm hug.

"Ah, tesoro, congratulations," he says, rubbing my back and giving me a kiss on the cheek.

Nonno does the same, wishing me well in Italian. I don't actually speak Italian despite being it. But I understand most of it, even if I can't actually make the pronunciations properly.

"So, what's this Daddy mentioned about a surprise?" I ask.

Uncle Tony rolls his eyes. "That man can't keep anything from you."

"You'll find out soon enough," Nonno says. "Go on and get ready, I saw some junior professor fussing about. That usually means it's almost showtime." He pats me on the back as I run off where the salutatorian and dean are, already prepared.

I hastily straighten my cap and gown and wait my turn, blushing at the wolf whistles from Daddy and Uncle Tony once I reach the podium. I can't see them, but everyone in a three-mile radius definitely heard them.

Public speaking is not exactly my forte, and I make it through my speech gritting my teeth during every pause.

It seems like ages until I receive my diploma, seeing as how Santini is fairly far down the alphabet. It's a big moment, for sure, but I still have to deal with law school come autumn. I am far from done, and this is just a waystation on my road to joining the family firm with the Santini men. I'll be the first female in the family to go to grad school, and the first woman in the family to join the firm.

That is worth celebrating.

After it is over, we all migrate to Gogi, on California Avenue, which is one of my favorite restaurants. Caleb and Uncle Tony aren't big fans of Korean food, but Mom shut Caleb up quickly when he started to whine.

"When you graduate college in only two years, you can pick the restaurant," Maggie teased him.

Inside, I spy the Choi twins with their family, already seated. But nobody looks happy as an older woman, their grandmother perhaps, scolds the whole table.

"Um, let's not sit near them," I suggest. "That lady is mad they weren't valedictorians. I'd like to not have her recognize me and drag me into their drama."

"You can understand them?" Mom asks.

"Oh yeah, they gave me lessons during school," I reply. "Did I not mention that?" I had mentioned it to the men, but it must have slipped my mind with Mom. Oops. That happens a lot lately.

Once seated, we order a few dishes family style, including bibimmyeon, my favorite, and of course bulgogi, plus all the amazing side dishes they provide.

It isn't until we finish eating that Daddy hands me a long, rectangular envelope. I wonder for a second if he got me the same gift Mom did: four-day VIP passes for Lollapalooza. It would be amusing to say the least.

"Something you mentioned a few times you wanted to do," he said. "I think you deserve a vacation."

It can't be, can it? I gingerly open the envelope and see ... four first-class tickets to Seoul! It's for a month, in August, and I startle the whole restaurant with my scream of delight.

Not thinking, I throw myself at Daddy, hugging him tightly. "That's amazing, thank you so so so much!"

I grin to myself as I take my seat again. A month in Seoul with all three of my men. What could be better?

Chapter Two

Sasha

BEFORE I CAN go on my trip, I have to start my summer internship. Which isn't so bad, seeing as how I intern at the family firm.

I mean, what's not to love? Interesting cases, sexy bosses, work experience.

Did I also forget to mention that the three men I'm dating are my ex-stepfamily? Shit. I need to get better at remembering the important stuff, don't I?

I managed to be able to stay with them for the summer, since of course

Mom knows nothing about this, by reminding her we often work after hours and it is closer and easier to stay there than go all the way to her neighborhood.

Someday I'm going to have to come clean. I hope that day will be at least after grad school ends, to give myself more time to figure everything out. It's easy to say I love all three and want to be with them all, but the reality is not so simple when, number one, alternative relationships aren't exactly accepted, and number two, I've known these men since I was five, and one was married to my mother.

I read a lot, and these books make it seem like it's easy for a girl to have a harem, but it's not. Not in the real world. There's a lot to navigate, not to mention, would we get married? Would

I just marry one of them? What if I want kids?

Yeah, I have a lot on my mind. I hope learning the ropes at work will clear it a bit. It was different at eighteen, life wasn't real yet, you know? But now I'm staring down reality, and the last thing I want is to get the firm in trouble for fucking all three of them.

No, not fucking. I am highly aware that I'm madly in love with all three, just as they are with me and each other. It's unconventional, many would say wrong, but we're happy.

That should be all that matters.

Santini and Sons Law Firm is located in a huge chunk of a high rise Nonno owns downtown. It's meant to feel imposing and it does. For defense attorneys, if a client is too much of a wimp to handle their attitudes and the decor, it shows them they would be a poor client anyway.

My heels click on the tiles as I exit the elevator, arriving later than the men so no one suspects anything odd going on between us. After greeting Allie, the other intern, I head right to Nonno's office, excitement bubbling in my veins. My first two years of internship were spent fetching files and brewing coffee. It was customary for all interns, and they couldn't show me preferential treatment.

This time, I'll actively assist on cases.

Maybe excitement is too light of a word. "Fucking ecstatic" might be better.

Inside Nonno's office, his secretary, Andrew, greets me.

"Miss Santini, welcome back," he says. "Mr. Santini Senior is in a last minute meeting, he told me to have you head to your stepfather's office, he'll have some work for you to complete."

"Thank you. And it's *ex-stepfather*," I correct.

"Apologies," he says, not at all apologetic.

"No worries."

Ugh. Between this guy's attitude and Mrs. DiFranco, the old bitch of a secretary Dad and Uncle Tony keep around, I'm going to need migraine medicine. Do they deliberately hire dicks? He's new, I should be nice, but I'm touchy about how people refer to my boyfriends.

I clickity-clack over to Daddy's office, saying good morning to other lawyers at the firm as I pass them in the halls. Some respond. Some turn their noses up at me. They don't realize I'm not here because I'm related to the men, sort of. I'm here because I'm damn good at what I do. That's proven by how I helped discover Uncle Tony was being stalked two years ago.

I knock on Daddy's office door and wait for him to say come in. The secretary station that sits before his and Uncle Tony's office doors is empty.

Inside his spacious but plain office, he sits behind his large oak desk, and Uncle Tony lounges on a guest chair. It must be a slow day for them.

"Secretary quit on you?" I ask as I close the door behind me.

"She'll be in later," Daddy replies. "Did you see Dad?"

"Meeting," I reply. "Secretary sent me here, he said you had work for me to do."

Daddy nods. "Yeah, new client. We'll probably get briefed later." He stands to his full nearly six feet of height, made more imposing by the fact that he's built like a tank. While all three have broad shoulders and dark eyes, Uncle Tony and Nonno are slender, whereas Daddy could be related to Jason Momoa. Or maybe Wonho.

Even in my heels, I come up to the tip of his nose.

He takes me by the waist and places me on top of Daddy's desk faster than I can react. The wood is hard under my ass and Daddy chuckles behind me.

"Did you think we wouldn't give you a first day welcome, little one?"

Heat extends from my face to my chest. It's not like I don't sleep with at least one of them nightly, but so far, they only touched me in the office once, and that was before I became an intern. They've been nothing but professional.

"What brought this on?" I ask. "Not that I'm complaining!"

Daddy's warm hands come on my shoulders from behind and he lays me back so my head is hanging off the desk and I'm looking up at him, my face level with his straining zipper.

"Grad school internships are more difficult and intense. We just wanted you to be as relaxed as possible," Uncle Tony explains.

"And to understand that you have more duties here than the ones on paper," Daddy adds. "You have to prove you're capable to your superiors."

Normally, a man saying that to me would leave him singing falsetto for at least an hour, but the way Daddy says it, my body gives an involuntary shiver.

In reality, I know I'm in control in this relationship. But I prefer it when they make me forget that.

Daddy tweaks my nipples from under my blouse and bra, squeezing my breasts in his hands. Meanwhile, Uncle Tony's strong hands spread my legs and my panties immediately vanish somewhere.

Daddy's still-clothed erection rubs against my face deliberately while Uncle Tony's thumb brushes my clit a few times, encouraging the wetness that has begun pooling between my legs.

I'm not sure what to do with my hands, so I lift my skirt more, helping Uncle Tony.

"Good girl," he praises. "Make it easier for me to violate your little cunt."

Daddy unzips his slacks and pulls his cock out, stroking it a few times before he brushes the tip across my lips, smearing precum on them. I lick it off and watch his cock twitch as he watches me.

"Give Daddy a kiss," he orders and I do so, pressing my lips to the tip of his cock, then along the shaft. He grabs me by the hair and holds me still. "Open up."

I open my mouth and he slowly slides inside. Not as thick as Uncle Tony, Daddy is long, hitting the back of my throat immediately. As I fight my gag reflex, Uncle Tony's cock pierces my pussy, moving in easily as he stretches me.

He fills me all the way up and holds himself there for a moment. Just as Daddy begins to move past my throat, Uncle Tony pulls out and slams back in, shoving me upwards, swallowing all of Daddy.

I panic for a moment and then remember to breathe through my nose as I hear both men chuckle at my discomfort.

"You'd think she never took my cock before," Daddy comments. "Every time you pretend to be innocent, we'll ruin you over and over again."

I whimper at his words as he fists my hair and moves back, letting me breathe for a second before he plunges back in.

At the same time, Uncle Tony begins to set his pace inside me, pulling my legs as far apart as they can go. His grip on my thighs is so tight, he'll be adding fresh bruises there. Not that he hasn't before.

They move alternately, and it's like I'm on a swing. Up, Daddy's in my throat. Down, Uncle Tony's impaling my cervix without remorse. I don't get a reprieve, and they don't speak anymore. The only sounds are their grunts and my wetness echoing around the office.

My breasts bounce hard, jolting me even more. Lucky I have on a tight corset under my blouse for the silhouette, or they'd be bouncing free or break the bra. It wouldn't be the first time.

I hear a click; Uncle Tony's taking pictures. Again, this is not the first time. The insides of all our phones look like we're porn photographers. One hack, our lives could be ruined. We should be scared, and I am, but the fear is also hot as fuck.

I'm so close to coming, but I can't in this position, and they know it, because they use me for as long as possible, leaving me on the edge with no way to fall. Finally, Uncle Tony presses his thumb to my clit and rubs hard, and I fall off the precipice into a blissful abyss.

Daddy comes down my throat with a grunt, and Uncle Tony pulls out of me at the same time he does. My body trembles from the aftershocks of my orgasm and I barely register Uncle Tony coming around to this side of the desk. He unbuttons the top three buttons of my blouse and comes down my shirt, into the dip of my corset's bra and on my breasts.

He rebuttons my blouse and they both tuck themselves back in as if nothing happened. Daddy helps me to sit up, and Uncle Tony takes me in his arms, licking Daddy's spilled come off my face before plunging his tongue into my mouth.

"Don't get used to this, tesoro," he warns as he pulls away. "We'll usually have to be much quicker than this. And for every time we come and you don't, we'll spoil you once we get home."

I hop off the desk and get steady on my legs. "That better be a promise."

Uncle Tony gently brushes his finger against my cheekbone. "Have we ever lied to you, tesoro?" He gives me a soft kiss where his finger was and my whole heart swells with love.

How did I get so lucky?

Daddy's phone buzzes and he presses speaker. "Yeah, Dad?"

"If you're done having fun with our girl, come meet me in my office. We can discuss the new case over early lunch," he says and hangs up.

It's already 11am. How long did we take?

Nonno's office is the largest, of course, and most beautifully decorated. He orders in and we all sit around the coffee table, waiting for him to tell us about his meeting.

"Last week," he begins, "did you all hear about the roadblock on the way into the city?"

I nod. "We had to turn around because of it."

"There was a body found," he continues. "Collin Gross, one of our former employees. His body was fairly fresh, perhaps two days gone. The scene was brutal. The police are sending photographs, but what they want from us is to go through cases he worked on with us and pick out any offenders who might be out to get him. His current firm is doing the same."

Daddy wipes his mouth and says, "He's been gone from here for nineteen years if I remember right. It would be one patient bastard to take that long."

"Or someone just released from prison," I say.

"As usual, she's right," Uncle Tony says. "Gene, you worked the most with him, right? Maybe you remember something off the top of your head?"

Daddy shakes his head. "Not right now, but I'll look. Baby," he turns his eyes on me, "you're going to help me. Consider it your first official duty this summer."

"Yes, sir," I reply lightly, enjoying how his pupils dilate.

"Don't start. I'm not even recovered yet," he warns, standing to throw his trash away.

"You don't have time. The cops will breathe down our necks if you don't hurry your culo up and search," Nonno warns.

Being defense attorneys, we're not exactly the local police's favorite people. Any chance they get to snoop in our files and building, they'll take it. All three men have different areas of expertise: business, entertainment, and sports. But all three have taken criminal defense cases.

When we exit Nonno's office and I follow Daddy to his, we're both dismayed and a little confused to see two uniformed officers standing outside it, faces dark as thunderclouds.

"Are you Mr. Eugene Santini?" one asks.

"And if I am?" he replies, smirking.

"Your secretary has gone missing."

Chapter Three

Gene

"WAIT, WHAT?" NO way I heard that right. My secretary is seventy-five and has worked here since before Tony and I were born. We kept her on after retirement age hit at her request because she loves "us boys" as she calls us, and wanted to stick around. I gave her the morning off with pay so Tony and I could have alone time with Sasha.

"Missus Mae DiFranco, widow; her grandson called us that she hadn't checked in on him since Saturday, and he was concerned. We did a wellness check and found no one at her residence," the officer explains. "We were informed she works here, and yet I do not see her."

"Because I gave her the morning off," I reply. "She should be in any minute now."

"When was the last time you spoke to her?" the second officer asks.

I pause. "When she left on Friday evening. That's when I told her to come in late today."

"Do you have any alternate contact information?"

The scoff leaves my mouth before I can stop it. "The lady uses a cell phone from the year two-thousand. Do you think she's on Tinder or Instagram?"

Behind me, Sasha chokes back a laugh. I don't turn to look at her. If I do, I may laugh, too, and the last thing one wants to do is laugh in a couple of cops' faces. Especially if they already don't like you.

"This is no joking matter, Mr. Santini," the first cop says. I can see the tips of his ears reddening and it takes all my willpower not to ask if he needs some ice for them.

"I don't believe it is," I reply. "But I cannot help you. If I hear anything, I will let you know. Now, if you don't mind, I have a law firm to run."

They leave with the sticks still firmly shoved up their asses, and I try to get back to work. Usually, I'm good at ignoring distractions. But Mrs. DiFranco going missing is not a run of the mill distraction.

I can't help but think about Collin, our old employee, found murdered. And now someone else who works here is missing.

Am I paranoid, or am I onto something?

Never in my life have I hoped for paranoia more.

An electronic file appears in my email, filled with details of Collin's case. The first thing I see when I click to open it is his staring face, eyes wide with terror, mouth and chin covered in dried blood. A closer image of his mouth shows that his tongue was cut out with what looks like a pair of scissors. The same scissors they say were recovered at the crime scene, having been used to cut his throat. He'd been sodomized with a tree branch. Most likely pre-mortem.

No fingerprints. DNA was inconclusive because all his blood contaminated anything they might have found.

"Who did you piss off?" I mutter. "Sasha, go down to the file room and request they locate and bring up any files that have not been digitized, please."

"Sure, Daddy," she replies, walking out with her heels clicking against the floor.

I shamelessly watch her until she closes the door behind her as she leaves. Moments still hit me that everything about my life is wrong. This four-way relationship is one big red flag, but I'm ... happy. I haven't really been happy since I was a kid, but I am now.

Our mother died when Tony and I were sixteen, and I don't think anything ever truly felt 'right' since then. A light went out, and obviously Sasha didn't relight something so maternal, but she brought a flashlight with her when she entered our hearts, and a place that had been dark in mine became illuminated again. I think it's the same with Tony and Dad, too.

I lean back in my chair, recalling how my brother and I started our, um, unconventional relationship, and what happened when Dad found out.

* * *

Tony's always been the more daring one compared with me. Yet one thing we had in common was being shy with girls in high school.

It was a week before senior prom when I found him angry at what looked to be his pillow. He was punching it half to death.

"Whoa!" I yelled when I walked into his bedroom, curious about the noise. "What did your bed do to you?"

He gave it one last punch and sat back on his haunches, huffing out a breath. "It never had anybody in it, that's what it did!"

I arched an eyebrow and shut the door as I walked into his room. Dad was at work, but still, we were eighteen and we wanted privacy. "I gotta ask, you always never specify girls. Do you like guys?"

He laughs and lays back on the now indented pillow. "We both do and you fucking know it, bro."

I did, but I wanted to hear him admit it. "I like girls more," I admit.

"Me too. But doesn't change a thing, because I haven't had either in here, and I'm going to prom with Marcy

Thomas. I've never even been sucked off; I'm gonna fucking embarrass myself."

I nod, sitting in his desk chair. Now his frustration makes sense. "Yeah. I'm going with Amy Horowitz. Same deal. And we all know she's experienced as fuck."

"I think even the school administrators know," he replies.

Yeah, that was probably accurate, now that I think about it. She graduated with some pretty shitty grades.

"What do we do?" I asked.

"Get experience, I guess," Tony replied.

I scoffed. "How do you propose we do that? We haven't had much luck so far." Which is even more amusing, considering we were good looking rich kids. But we didn't act like they did, all fake confidence and swagger. Maybe that was it.

I don't know what the fuck happened. I blacked out or just blinked, and the next thing I knew, Tony was on the floor, on his knees in front of me, one hand on my belt.

"The fuck are you doing? Are you high?" I asked.

But I didn't push him away.

"We both like men, and we're twins. We might not look alike, but we both know what each other has. This is the surest way to get some experience with minimal risk." Tony sounded like Dad, talking about risks and speaking in that calm tone.

This time I did grab his wrist, holding him in place. "We're brothers."

"Right. We can't get pregnant, there's no risk here. Just reward." He broke my already weak hold and unbuckled my belt. My cock surged in my pants and I felt like my tongue weighed ten pounds. I couldn't move it to protest anymore as my zipper became undone and my twin grabbed my cock, bringing it out to see.

"We shouldn't..." I didn't finish my protest as Tony licked the head and I nearly saw stars. "Fuck me."

"That too, eventually," he replied as he licked me again.

I'll be honest, sex between two complete novices is not hot. It's just not. That first blowjob lasted all of two minutes before I made Tony choke on my cum. And when I returned the favor, I think he came sooner than I did.

But the feeling of societal wrongness, the essence of the taboo, was like a drug for us. Over the next two weeks, we tried everything we could think of. Which, for teenagers, is pretty much sucking and fucking.

I'm quiet, and Tony is loud. And one afternoon that summer as I fucked him in my bed, he was yelling obscenities and begging me to let him come when we heard the door slam downstairs.

I've never seen my brother shut up so fast in my life. And I don't think either of us purposefully ever finished so fast in case Dad came upstairs and we got caught.

Confident we covered our tracks, we cleaned up and went downstairs to start dinner, since Dad was home early.

It wasn't until we were all seated in the living room, drinking espresso and having dessert, that we discovered how wrong we were.

Dad muted the news and turned towards us. "How long have you been fucking?"

I nearly choked on a piece of tiramisu and drained my espresso to clear my airways before I died. "What?"

Tony was silent. Again, weird for him.

"It's a simple question: when did this begin?" he asked, not letting us look away with his sharp gaze.

Fuck fuck fuck, I thought. *Do I laugh? Do I deny?*

But my fucking brother didn't let me finish making a decision as he said, "Two weeks before prom."

"Dude!" I groaned.

"Eugene, you're going to need to learn to be confident in responding if you want to even make it to law school," Dad scolded. "If you were going to lie, you should've lied easily and calmly, not looked like a rabbit in a trap.

"And Anthony, that blunt nature will intimidate opponents, but maybe next time at least consider lying first." Dad put his cup on the coffee table, calm as could be.

I was certain he was going to beat both our asses. We'd never been hit growing up bar some light smacks with Mom's wooden spoon when we tried to sneak food before dinner. But I had no idea how to interpret the look on his face. It had to be rage, right? Disgust, maybe?

I was afraid to find out, but knew it was coming.

"Well?" I asked, ready to get it over with.

"Show me."

"Excuse me?" Tony and I said at the same time. I was hearing things, right?

"You heard me. Don't make me say it twice." I knew that look on Dad's face. He was dead fucking serious.

And for some reason, my cock was rock fucking hard. A quick glance at Tony showed me his was too.

We were already in this far, right? What did it matter if we damned our souls a little bit more? Hell was Hell, and Tony and I were already headed there.

I pulled my brother by the back of the head and tongue kissed him, sucking his tongue into my mouth.

His hands gripped at my jeans and he fumbled because he was too busy kissing me to get a proper grip on my belt. Finally he got it open and his hot hand pulled my cock out, while I reached over and did the same to him.

We had nothing to prepare ourselves with, so I didn't suspect this was going to last long.

I glanced out the corner of my eye and saw Dad lean back in the chair, bulge evident in his pants, and nearly came then and there.

What the fuck is wrong with me? I wondered, but knew I'd never truly get an answer. But as long as I kept feeling this good, who gave a fuck?

I shoved Tony's hands away and muttered, "Hands off. Let me handle this."

He obeyed and I spat in my hand before taking both our cocks together. He was thicker than me, and that made it a bit difficult, but I held us both and began stroking up and down, rocking my hips in time with my hand.

I felt the heat in my stomach right before I came, and Tony followed on my heels, staining our shirts and probably pants. Hell, probably the expensive throw rug we're kneeling on.

We didn't get a chance to catch our breath before Dad spoke.

"Come here."

We turned to look at him, and he was still in the same position with a tent pitched in his slacks. Quickly, Tony and I glanced at each other. Fraternal twins don't have telepathy, but it's close enough when we look into each other's eyes. And while we were both apprehensive, we were also curious as fuck, and still half hard.

We walked over to Dad, whose eyes belied his calm expression.

"Kneel."

We both did as Dad began to undo his buckle and fly.

This was insane. I knew it was insane, but I was equally insane and wasn't going to say a word to stop any of it. It felt like I was under a spell, and I think Tony felt the same way.

None of us knew how we got here, but we did, and when Dad pulled his cock out, he didn't have to say a word before my twin and I got to work.

We licked the head at the same time, turning it into a heated kiss atop Dad's cock. Meanwhile, we grabbed each other's cocks as they began to harden again — I still miss being able to recover that quickly.

Dad's strong hands gripped both of our heads as he thrust his hips up, practically masturbating on our faces.

"Fuck, I never knew I raised such filthy boys," he said, his voice strained. "You really like this?"

In response, we both moaned as he pulled our hair harder.

I took my free hand and stroked him while Tony and I licked at the head, and right below, that little spot at the base of the head that feels like Heaven when its tongued.

And when Dad came, we both licked and swallowed as much as we could, and knew nothing was ever going to be quite the same again.

* * *

You'd think I couldn't complicate my life any more than that, right? Then I started fucking my stepdaughter and somehow wound up in a four-way relationship with her, my twin, and my father.

I'm not sure if this is the plot of a dirty novel or an episode of *Maury*.

As I think that, my door opens and Sasha pokes her head in. "Daddy, some staff is bringing all the boxes and I told them to leave them by the secretary's desk so as not to clutter up your office. Is that all right?"

"Perfect, baby. Thank you."

By the time all the boxes are brought up, it's time to leave. I know we need to find case files that might have gotten Collin killed, but it is Sasha's first day at work and the poor thing is exhausted. We can begin tomorrow.

We all carpool except Sasha, who insists she doesn't want to ride with us every day, lest someone wonder why she's apparently living with us, so we all head down to the employee underground garage together.

It's there I see a familiar car, and I know Dad and Tony see it, too. An old, beat to shit gold Lincoln.

"Is that..." Tony trailed off.

"That's not good," I comment.

"What?" Sasha asks.

"Mrs. DiFranco's car. I guess the cops didn't check the garage," Dad comments, holding Sasha by the shoulders. We all know what we're going to find, and he doesn't want her to have to see it.

I can already see the outline of a person behind the wheel, head slumped over.

God, if she's dead, please let it have been natural causes, I pray as I walk over to her car. Taking the handkerchief out of my suit pocket, I try the driver's side door, which opens. Her whole car seems unlocked, and the locks are all manual.

As soon as I do, her heavy body tumbles out, glasses askew and head tilted too far back to be normal, revealing a long, sharp slit in her throat. Her ruffled white blouse is drenched in sticky, stale blood, and the copper smell of it hits my nose, making me want to retch.

"I ... think we should call the police," Tony says weakly.

Mae DiFranco is dead.

And between her and Collin, that means someone is out to get the Santini law firm.

Chapter Four

Sasha

I WATCH THE dead body tumble out of the driver's seat in mute horror. It isn't my first corpse. No, that honor goes to my best friend when my ex killed her right in front of me.

But still, I am not exactly prepared to get used to seeing dead bodies anytime soon. At least, I hope I don't have to get used to it. We don't often take murder cases here anyway.

Daddy stares and shakes his head. "We'll prepare security camera footage for you to peruse," he tells the police officers who showed up rather quickly.

Her coagulating blood leaks out on the concrete floor due to her new position half out of the car and half still inside. It's slow, sluggish, and reminds me of thick syrup when you first open the bottle, or maybe organic honey.

Is that what vampires think when they drink it?

"Sasha, come this way," Uncle Tony says, turning me away from the gruesome sight.

"Looks like you and Eugene need a new secretary," Nonno comments.

"Oh, how sad." I roll my eyes.

"The words are right, but the tone isn't," he tells me, giving me a mildly worried look.

"That old hag treated me like shit whenever your back was turned the last two years. I'm not sorry someone finally found her throat under all those chins and slit it."

"Fuck, bambino, not so loud!" Nonno shushes.

"Why didn't you say anything?" Uncle Tony asks.

I shrug. "Dunno. I'm not that petty and she seethed every time I didn't take her bait anyway."

"Next time someone even looks at you the wrong way, you tell us. Understood?" Nonno says sternly.

"Yes, sir," I reply.

"Good girl." He looks over my shoulder and I hear a zipper. They must be loading up old DiFranco into a body bag. Hopefully that means we can go home.

Daddy joins us and rests his chin atop my head. "This is bad. And between her and Collin..."

"It seems like someone's targeting this company," I pipe up. "Weren't you guys just stalked because of me two years ago? This is redundant."

Uncle Tony chuckles. "Honey, this is real life, not the plot of a crime show. Sometimes things happen more than once."

"But stalking and murder?"

"Especially those," Nonno says. "We see it all the time."

"I'd rather see it in cases than our own backyard," I reply, crossing my arms. Shit, I really don't like this. If Collin was the only one dead, I'd think it was just him the killer was after. But now another employee... How long would it be before the next ones killed were me, or one of the men?

A chill goes down my spine, and Daddy pulls me closer as I give a shiver.

How do we know we're not being watched right now? Someone could be under a car, or inside one, and we'd have no idea.

That's it, no more horror movies before bed.

"You realize this doesn't look good, Santini," one of the officers says to Daddy as they walk past.

"No, it doesn't, considering we could be next," Daddy comments pointedly.

They want to make us think we could be suspects, but they're failing to see we're more likely to be victims.

The officer stammers, unable to get a full sentence out.

"Very intelligent," Nonno comments. "If you need anything from us, or have any information, please call and ask for my secretary, Andrew.

Otherwise, we'd prefer it if you did your jobs instead of harping on us."

"Of course, Mr. Santini. If you all see or hear anything strange, give us a call as well and ask for me." He nods and walks away at a brisk pace, obviously embarrassed. Good. He should be.

Why are lawyers considered the bad guys, when all the cops do is focus on the most obvious person instead of, y'know, actually investigating?

* * *

We heard nothing more by Friday that week, except that the likely weapon that killed DiFranco was a letter opener.

Collin Gross was killed with scissors. Now a letter opener. These almost seemed like crimes of passion rather than premeditated. But I think that's because we're supposed to think that. The killer is picking their weapons on purpose to confuse everyone. Or they work at an office supply store.

Ugh. Smart killers are only fun when they're not after you and your family.

"We have to get to the bottom of this shit before August first. I am not missing out on my trip to Seoul," I say during dinner Friday night.

"Maybe it's for the best," Uncle Tony comments. "You'll wind up meeting one of those band boys and leave us."

I slip out of my chair and into his lap, nipping at his lower lip. "Nope. I'm one of the rare and lucky fangirls who has men she loves more than K-pop boys."

"Lucky us we found you first," Daddy comments.

"You mean lucky you Uncle Tony basically kidnapped me first," I correct.

"That ... sounds bad when said out loud," Nonno says. "Don't do that anymore."

I get off Uncle Tony's lap and begin to help clear the table. "What, you don't think it rivals a meet-cute?"

"More like a 'meet the local prison' situation," Daddy says.

"I don't see either of your sorry asses complaining," Uncle Tony says.

"Well, no," Nonno says. "None of us are. But facts are facts."

I roll my eyes at their banter and load the dishwasher. "Come on, we have to get ready and meet the Chois for trip planning. The club they asked us to meet at is supposed to be pretty wild, so I'd like to get there earlier and have fun."

In my room, I put on a red silk minidress, black sparkly heels, and black panties before doing my hair up and putting on a backless bra to hold me in place. After playing with my makeup a little, I meet the men back in the living room. Walking down the stairs, I get whistles and catcalls.

They see me every day, and still know how to make me blush. And they look good themselves in form-fitting slacks and silk shirts. Simple is sexy on the right guy.

The club we arrive at is tucked away in Wicker Park, and the old building's exterior does not give away the neon and chrome inside. There are dancers, not strippers, but actual dancers, in skimpy clothes in cages in the corners, and star-shaped tables are strategically placed around a currently empty stage, also star-shaped. The lights flashed in shades of blue and purple, occasionally white, and gave the whole place an outer space vibe.

This was why I wanted to come early, to check out the dancers and have a good time with my men. After the tense week we had, we need it. I still wonder why the twins texted and told me not to come earlier than planned. What is the problem?

We get drinks, and no one cards me, which I am perfectly fine with, and I drag Uncle Tony to dance when "Left and Right" starts playing, switching men as each new song comes on.

The only one who dances well is Uncle Tony, but that doesn't matter.

This is fun. This is freeing. This is exactly what I wanted.

We eventually get more drinks and sit down at a table near the back. It seems like there's a dance show about to start, which should last right up until we have to meet the Chois.

Sure enough, the music changes and the lights dim, with spotlights only on the biggest stage in the center of the room.

But when both Chois walk out wearing next to nothing, I'm fucking speechless.

Not that they're not hot as Hell. They are. If I was single, I would have probably wanted to date them both. They have lithe dancers' bodies, which makes sense now that I see them in skimpy clothes that match their hair colors.

They begin to dance, and I had no idea either of them were this talented, or this flexible.

They look so elegant, so ethereal, like the fae in books I've read. The dances they do are sensual and highly honed. They must have taken lessons since they were little kids. I feel insanely proud of my friends, and then the song changes.

As the sexy, neo-soul beat plays, my mouth drops to see them kiss onstage. Like ... how many freaks are out here like my men? Is it a twin thing? And why do I find this insanely hot?

Looking at my guys, they find it hot too. I should be jealous they're looking at other people instead of me, but how can I be when I'm looking, too? And there is a lot to look at as Daniel removes Diana's bra and begins to play

with her breasts while she wraps her
legs around his waist and uses him like a
pole.

I can totally understand now why
they didn't want us to come early. I'm
sure they must think I'd judge them.
Little do they know!

Nonno pulls me into his lap, and I
can feel his hardness under my ass as I
deliberately wiggle against him.

Daddy and Uncle Tony tease me
under my skirt from either side as we
watch the Choi twins begin to make out
more as Diana strokes Daniel through
his blue sequined speedo.

"I don't think I'm in the mood to
plan a trip right now," I say to the guys,
making my voice audible above the
music.

Nonno grinds me down and says,
"I agree. Text your friends, have them

meet us tomorrow. We have more important things to deal with tonight."

Chapter Five

Nonno

SASHA'S PRETTY LITTLE friends were surprising last night, but pleasantly so considering how turned on it made Sasha. Our little girl has grown in confidence and no longer frets over how wrong our relationship is. Rather, she's more comfortable with it than my sons are half the time.

Me? I'm too old to give a fuck what others might think. My boys had freedom of choice, and … well, Sasha was strong-willed enough to have walked away if she wanted to. And she chose to stay.

I'm grateful she did. I took on many lovers since my wife passed away far too young. However, I never fell in love. I didn't believe I could, until Sasha was actually in my arms, and knelt before me. At that moment I knew my heart wasn't dead after all. It only took over twenty-five years, but I would go through all the grief again if I knew what awaited me at the end of that long, dark tunnel.

Though she usually drives herself to work, she agreed to come with us in our carpool that morning, probably too tired to drive from the night before. Indeed, she fell asleep on the ride there, and was groggy as we had to wake her to get her out of the car. Couldn't be seen carrying our intern, after all.

We usually make it a point to arrive before everyone else, to showcase a good worth ethic to our employees. I see two cars already in our part of the lot; I have no idea whose, however.

"The Chois are here early," Sasha comments, yawning. "The red one is Diana's car."

"I think they're still inside. Probably weren't sure where to go or anything to wait," Gene says.

Sasha smiles. "I'll go startle them." She walks over to their car, and I admire her ass from behind. She knocks on the window, then knocks harder. I can see the twin in the driver's seat's head thunk lifelessly against the window, and she screams.

"Ay cazzo," I mutter.

"No fucking way..." Tony rushes over and just in time, as Sasha loses her footing and nearly collapses.

Gene and I follow, and it's clear as day Diana is dead in the car, her head lolling unnaturally with a broken neck. I walk around the car and see Daniel, his blue hair matted with blood. On this side of the car, I can see where part of the fight and double homicide took place. There's blood on the marker for the parking spot; I'm assuming that's where Daniel got his head bashed in.

"Eugene," I call. "Get over here."

He comes around my side and I can hear Tony comforting a crying Sasha. We should do the same, but right now we need to get some shit done before the police arrive.

"Is that what I think it is?" I ask him.

He bends down and nods. "A loogie. Still not dried, so this happened not too long ago."

"It could be Daniel's. He was on this side," I begin.

"But it could also be the killer's," Gene finishes for me. He reaches for his handkerchief in his pocket and wipes some of it up, leaving some on the ground. "Our testing will come back faster than the cops'," he says, carefully folding the handkerchief up so the DNA didn't get contaminated.

"The killer..."

Sasha's weak voice shocks us as we turn and see her, Tony's arms protectively around her shoulders.

"The only way the killer would know the Chois were connected to us is if they followed us around last night, to the club," she finishes. I can visibly see her tremble. "They're getting closer to us, and not even our friends are safe."

She squeezes her eyes shut, obviously trying not to break down.

"Eugene, take her inside and get that thing off to our lab," I say. "Anthony and I have it here.

"But—"

"No," Gene interrupts Sasha. "You will not stay and see any more than you already have. Come on, with me." He takes her from Tony and kisses her head before leading her inside.

"That thing?" Tony questions.

"We may have found the killer's DNA," I explain, gesturing to the floor. "If we find them before the police do, then we can call someone and have it taken care of. Leave the corpse as a nice present for the police as a thank you for the bullshit work they claim they do."

The police arrive, and as I expected, they do nothing of note or

importance beyond notifying the Chois'
family and carting the bodies away. At
least they actually took the DNA from
the ground as I suggested.

The detective asks, "Why were
they here?"

"They're school friends of Sasha
Santini, and they were coming to help
her plan a trip," I reply. "I'm sure you'll
see the text messages on their phones."

"And why would someone after
your firm kill them?" he wonders.

"Because they're connected to us?
I can't answer that, Detective. Only the
killer can. And the longer you sit here
bothering me, the longer it will take for
you to find them. So might I suggest you
go do your job before more people in
this building wind up dead?"

The detective's eyes lit up. "So
you do believe there's a connection?"

"Collin Gross, former employee. Mae DiFranco, employee for forty-five years. Daniel and Diana Choi, longtime friends of our intern for the past two years. Yes, I do fucking believe there's a connection, and if you don't, you're more of a stunad than you look."

Tony muffles a laugh behind me.

"You know, Mr. Santini, you defend some pretty rotten people. It comes as a shock to no one that you're being targeted. Look at the company you keep." The detective sneers.

"Better than keeping company with the likes of you. Good day, and don't come back unless you have pertinent information," I say.

"Or unless another body drops," he calls over his shoulder.

"Fucking stronzo," I mutter, knowing he can hear me.

"We should go check on Sasha," Tony says. "And get to work finding potential cases."

I must agree. I can't let my anger cause me to not help take care of our little one.

As we go inside, some people who work on the other floors in the building give us a wide berth. We're marked, like we have scarlet letters pinned to our chests. Like we're walking targets, and anyone who gets too close might get caught in the crossfire as well.

For all I know, they're right.

Upstairs, Gene is working at the empty secretary desk. It will feel odd for quite some time to have Mrs. DiFranco not here with us. She's been here as long as we've been open.

"Sasha's asleep in my office," he says. "I'm ready to send off the DNA.

She asked for hers to be the sample to test against. I think maybe it makes her feel like she's helping her friends."

I nod. Our Sasha is a sweet girl with a heart far bigger than anyone I've ever known. And she has been through far too much lately.

"Go take it to the lab and then help your brother sort the cases, while I get started on anything electronic, just in case." But first, I am going to check on Sasha.

She's asleep, curled into herself on the small loveseat in Gene's office, but she's not sleeping well. Her body jerks and she whimpers. Whether it's because of the Chois' murders or if she's reliving the horror she went through two years ago, I don't know.

Sitting down, I gently lift her so her head is in my lap. She rouses a bit and wraps one arm around me as well as she can, making her body as small as possible.

I stroke her hair and her back, fighting off emotions I had no idea I was still able to feel.

"You deserve a better life than this, cara," I whisper. "I am so sorry. But you're strong, and we're here with you. I promise, everything will be okay."

* * *

Remind me to never make promises again.

The DNA results come in the next day, and I volunteer to go pick them up. The middle aged woman working that desk is vaguely familiar, but I usually don't come in personally.

"Well, you got an easy one this time," she says to me as I sign for the DNA testing results. She slides a manila file across the desk to me.

Whatever that means, I think, putting it in my briefcase. I thank her and get on my way, hoping she meant the killer's DNA was in the public system, not the police database, so we can catch this motherfucker.

When I get back, I alert Gene, Tony, and Sasha to come to my office.

They gather around, Sasha and Gene on the sofa, Tony in one of the plush armchairs, while I sit at my desk, looking for my letter opener. I sigh, figuring Allie, the other intern, or Andrew, my secretary, used it and didn't put it back in the proper place.

"Here." Sasha offers me her pocket knife, which I use and hand back to her.

I pull out the results and see a red "MATCH" stamped on the paper. They did find a match. For a moment, I allow myself to feel hopeful. Then I see what the match is.

The DNA from the crime scene matches Sasha's.

Chapter Six

Gina

PEOPLE THINK I'M cold, and that's because I am. But one thing I am as well is a good mother. I know my kids like the back of my hand, which is why, when Sasha calls me instead of texting, I know it's an emergency. Despite being in the middle of a consultation, I tell my client to hold on and pick up the phone.

"Sash? Is everything all right?"

"No, Mom, it's not. You need to come down to the law firm," she replies. Her voice is hard, but I can hear a tremble underneath the ice.

"Are you all right? Gene?"

"Physically, we're all fine. But you need to come down here immediately or there's a chance I'm going to jail tonight."

Excuse me? I pause, unable to speak. My baby, in jail? No. She'd never do anything wrong, not like that.

"I'll be right there."

One good thing about my new promotion, I only have one person to answer to, and the second I tell her one of my kids has an emergency, she clears my schedule so I can go down there and figure out what's going on.

I don't think Anthony Senior ever liked me much, and the distaste on his face is evident when I walk into his office, which is as big as our living and dining rooms combined at home. It looks like he could live here.

Sasha sits on the couch between Gene and Tony, while Anthony Senior sits on one of the plush armchairs across the coffee table from the sofa.

"Gina," he greets. "Have a seat."

I don't, I stand in front of Sasha, my back to him, and ask, "What's going on? What did you mean you might go to jail? What did you do?"

Sasha shakes her head, a weary smile on her face. "Seriously, Mom? What did I do? I didn't do anything! But this says I did." She points to a manila file on the coffee table. I recognize the logo from my years married to Gene: it's a DNA testing lab. He'd often go there for independent results while working a case.

"May I?" I ask before reaching for it. Who knows, it could be classified.

"Go ahead," Gene says, gently rubbing Sasha's back. He always treated her like his own child, which I appreciated then and still do.

Picking up the file, I try to make sense of the medical jargon. Sample 1 and sample 2 are a match. Sample 2 has Sasha's name written on it.

"What is this for?" I ask.

"The murders we've been looking into. The attorney who worked here, Collin, Mrs. DiFranco, and the Choi twins. The police found DNA at the scene of their murder, and they haven't run it yet," Tony explains. "Or they ran it and it hasn't come back. Either way... We obtained a sample for ourselves, and ran it. As always, we have one of us put our DNA in as something to go off. This time, Sasha volunteered. And it came back a match."

"Obviously she didn't—"

"No shit, Mom," Sasha interrupts. "But someone closely related to me did. Either Maggie or Caleb, which I highly doubt, one of your relatives you don't talk to, or someone related to my father."

At that last word, my legs turn to jelly and I plop down in the chair originally offered to me.

"Why do I get the feeling you lied when you said you didn't know who Sasha's father was?" Gene asks me.

Anthony Senior gets up and brings me a cold bottle of water.

I thank him as I uncap it and take a sip, trying not to tremble.

"Mom, are you okay?" Sasha's dark eyes widen as she looks at me.

"No. Yes. Fuck if I know." I rarely curse. Letting that slip out is very telling.

"This might be difficult, especially since you've covered it up for twenty years, but you have to tell us everything you know. Our girl's future and freedom are at stake," Anthony Senior says quietly.

"This ... isn't something Sasha should hear," I say.

"I disagree," she replies. "And it would take a bulldozer to move me out of this room. I am related to a serial killer and rapist, Mom. This is fucking serious. There's no time to spare my feelings."

I sip more water and sigh. It's not like I don't still think about what happened. I do. Far too often for my tastes. But I never told another soul, not even my family, not even when they kicked me out for getting pregnant at eighteen and unmarried.

"If I tell you, none of you can judge me for lying about it," I say, trying to hold my head up high despite the fact I feel less than confident.

"You did what you had to do for you and for Sasha," Gene says. "None of us would judge you for that."

I sigh, knowing I don't have much of a choice but to tell the truth. And hope that the one thing I clearly recall can help Sasha now.

His name. I know his name.

* * *

January 2002

Being winter in Chicago, the school bus was more crowded than usual. No one wanted to walk home, even though it was a comfortable thirty degrees and not the usual below zero we got in January.

The walk home was a mile, but it seemed preferable to riding the hot, smelly bus. Especially since the track team was on the one that would take me home.

Gross.

Plus, in Chicago, gangways and alleys aren't like what you think about in cities. They're usually shoveled and plowed and salted, so they're safe to walk down. And as it was getting dark, I also knew the lights would be bright in the alleys and the ground freshly salted. My legs would get cold since I didn't put on my wool tights that morning, but oh well. I'd live.

Never knew I'd wish I rode the bus, that it would wind up my biggest regret.

Halfway home, my shoelace came undone. You'd think it would be ice that tripped me, right? No, my stupid shoelace.

I yelped as I started to go down, when two strong hands grabbed me under each arm, holding me partway up before I hit the ground.

"You all right, hon?" a man asked.

I turned around and straightened my askew coat. He was dressed like a civilian, but I saw a badge at his hip, which he quickly covered.

"Yes, thanks, Officer," I said. "That was close." I knelt down and fixed my shoelace.

"Lucky for you I'm doing plainclothes patrols here and not in my cruiser. I never would've caught you in time," he commented. "Where do you live? Far from here?"

I calculated. "Half a mile. I walk it all the time." I didn't, but he didn't need to know that.

"It's getting dark, and my jurisdiction extends another full mile. Let me walk you home, please."

I glanced up at him. He wasn't bad looking, I guess. I wasn't into older guys, and he was maybe thirty. Could still even be a rookie, given that he was working a beat in such a boring neighborhood as mine.

"Ah, sure. Why not?" I said. "Thank you." *If I tell Mom about this, she's going to have my wedding planned to this dude,* I thought.

"You can lead the way," he said, taking me by the upper arm, I guess in case I fell again.

As I said, the alleyway was well lit from the apartments, and most of the parking lot was empty, seeing as how it was mid-afternoon on a Tuesday. Every few buildings, there would be two huge dumpsters. In between the dumpsters were large piles of freshly shoveled snow from the night before, still mostly gleaming white, frozen into large, solid blocks.

We walked for maybe two city blocks while he asked me the usual inane questions high school students get — how old I was, what year I was in, what my college plans were, all that crap I hated being asked. Eighteen. Senior. I wanted to go into fashion design. My parents wouldn't let me.

Mid-sentence, as we passed one of the large snow piles, he shoved me away from him. I landed on the snow, breaking my fall.

"What the fuck?" I cried, going to get up, but I was too slow in my surprise, and the snow was slightly slippery.

As I scrambled, he was on me in a second, fully prepared. He'd planned this. And while a minute ago, I was nearly a hundred percent sure he was a real cop, there was a tiny part of me that wondered if I'd been totally scammed.

It didn't matter. What was about to happen was going to happen no matter what.

"Stop!" I cried, only to be hit upside the head, making me dizzy.

He unzipped my coat and tore my school blouse with one hand, trapping my arms in the coat sleeves so I could only move them a little bit forward, not enough to try and hit him. The cold hit me and my nipples pebbled before his rough hand grabbed my breasts, heaving them out of the bra.

He punched them and I gasped in pain, which made him laugh.

"Knowing it hurts makes me harder," he commented. "Now, you're going to not scream, not cry, or I'll take my gun and make a new hole for me to fuck. Understood?"

My whole body felt numb with fear. I had no idea that could even happen. I wasn't even sure he had a gun, or that the badge was real, but was I going to take that risk?

He slapped me across the face. "Answer, bitch!"

"Y-yes," I whispered, tasting blood in my mouth where my teeth snagged the corner of my lip during the hit.

He put one hand around my throat, the other snaked under my school skirt and tore at my panties, the elastic ripping and snapping against my thighs as he tore them away.

Two rough fingers entered me and I gasped again. No one ever touched me before. And his fingers were bigger than mine by far.

"Please..." I said, trying not to cry.

His hand closed harder around my throat and I couldn't talk anymore. He moved back and the next thing I knew, there was searing, burning pain between my legs as his cock entered me. Even if I wasn't scared to scream, the pain was so bad I couldn't make any noise at all.

He held me still at the waist with one hand, and the one on my throat moved to my breasts again, squeezing and scratching with his blunt nails. All the while, his vile cock stabbed my insides over and over.

And then, to me, the absolute worst thing happened.

I came.

I came and bucked on a cock that was raping me. Intellectually, I know it was just an involuntary reaction, but it was still the deciding factor in my never telling a soul what happened.

That was the part I hated the most, and still do.

He laughed as he fucked me through my orgasm. "Little virgin cunt likes it, doesn't it? All you religious girls are sluts in disguise. It's a wonder you weren't raped before this, bitch." He slammed into me harder and added, "Hold still, you're about to get the best present a worthless thing like you will ever receive."

And he thrust harder than before, burying himself as deep as possible before hot cum filled me up.

I felt faint, and dizzier than before, and in pain. Before I passed out, as he pulled out and started to buckle his pants, I saw his badge again. It wasn't a police badge, rather it was for a rent-a-cop.

I saw his name.

Tomassi.

Chapter Seven

Sasha

WANT TO vomit. Cry. Run away. But I do none of that because, while learning what I did about myself is awful, I'm not the one who went through trauma. That was Mom, and she doesn't need me running away to nurse my wounds when she just ripped hers open and bled all over the Persian rugs.

"Oh my God, Mom..."

"No," she says, wiping her eyes. "No pity."

"Not pity, *empathy*," I retort, perhaps a bit snottier than intended. "You're not the only one who has been through that in this room, and I wish you'd talked to me sooner."

Daddy speaks up. "I'm sorry, Gina."

"About what?" Now Mom looks less upset, more puzzled.

"Had I known, many arguments would have been avoided," he explains.

"Too late for regrets. Now, if you don't mind, I have to go back to work. Did you get what you needed from me to stop Sasha going to prison?"

She's ignoring me now, after my admission. I'm sure she'll mull it over, possibly even for a week or more, before she brings it up again. And that's fine. I'd rather not talk about just how many times Trevor forced me ... or tell her what happened in that basement two years ago.

"Yes," Nonno says. "Though you may be called to testify if need be. But it all depends if we find the actual bastard and how long he lives."

Mom nods and stands up, screwing her face into the mask I've seen all my life.

"You know I'm here if you need me, but I truly hope you don't."

As she leaves, I finally sag, holding my head in my hands.

What the actual fuck is my life?

"Sasha?" Uncle Tony says softly, and I feel his warm hand on my back.

"That was a lot," Daddy says. "If you need a few minutes..."

"No." I push my hair from my face and sigh. "I can't believe... No wonder she was so cold a lot of the time towards me. I was a reminder of—"

"No," Daddy practically growls. I didn't know people did that in real life! "Do not blame yourself or your existence. Your mother chose to keep you, and she chose to raise you. That was on her to not let how you came to be cloud her mind, because she made that choice. It's not on you, baby."

"But I'm related to—"

It is Nonno's turn to interrupt me. They never do that, so for two of them in a row to do it, I know they are serious.

"None of that, little one. My father was a good for nothing deadbeat ... and he lived with us! I vowed to never be anything like him, and I'm not. And you're obviously nothing like yours. So don't you even start to worry about nature versus nurture." His eyes are like black steel under his eyebrows and I shiver.

He is dead serious, and I know I have to listen to him. He isn't blowing smoke up my ass just because he loves me. Neither is Daddy.

Uncle Tony sits back and pulls me with him, cuddling me to his chest. I love him, love them all, so damn much it hurts. I'm safe here, with them. Nothing can touch me, or so it feels like.

But something can touch them, as they are my first and only line of defense.

What if the police find my DNA is a match and don't believe it's another person? It wasn't like there was semen, it was saliva they recovered. They're going to need alibis, and whenever I am not studying, which I'm not right now, I am with them. That's ... a little suspect.

And the cops hate my family for obvious reasons. So what if? What if they dig deeper and discover we're all in a relationship? Bad enough they're my former stepfamily. But Daddy and Uncle Tony and Nonno… They'll be ruined. What they have hurts no one, but that doesn't matter in this world.

I can't let that happen.

I gently run my hand down Uncle Tony's abs. What I am about to do is gonna hurt me, and them, but I need them all relaxed. And there's one easy way to do that.

"Can you please make me feel better?" I ask quietly. "All three of you?"

We'd been so focused on individual dates, the four of us haven't been together for a while now. But now I need it. Ulterior motive or not, I need it. I need to feel like something more than a gross little slug, which is how the truth of my very being now makes me feel.

"Anything for you," Uncle Tony whispers. His fingers caress my face and neck, a butterfly-light touch. They trail down the front of my blouse, undoing buttons as they go.

From behind, either Daddy or Nonno lift my skirt and when the panties are torn away, I know it's Daddy.

Nonno's office is much more comfortable than Daddy's, that's for sure. Uncle Tony lays back and brings me on top of him on the plush sofa, my bare ass now in the air. He kisses me slowly as Daddy coats his cock in the wetness gathering between my legs.

I feel hands between us as Nonno undoes Uncle Tony's pants, freeing his cock, before he comes to stand by my face. Bending down it's his turn to kiss me just as I feel Daddy's cock at the entrance of my ass.

My body stiffens; I'm probably loose from last night, but still...

I gasp as he pushes inside, and as my mouth opens, Nonno puts his cock inside, stopping any more sound from emitting. Unlike the twins, Nonno prefers I do most of the work, which honestly is hot as Hell to me. He's in control, and he wants me to work for what I need. So I suck hard, taking him as far as he lets me in his current position.

Meanwhile, Uncle Tony pushes gently into my pussy. Well, gentle for him. He's being uncharacteristically sweet; I am not sure if I like it or not. He starts to kiss and suck at my neck as he and Daddy find a pace they both like, moving alternately inside me like machines.

None of us can come quickly in this position, which was what I was hoping for. The longer this lasts, the more tired they'll be.

"I could stay like this forever," Uncle Tony whispers, gripping my waist tighter, ensuring I will be bruised tomorrow. That makes me shiver. I love having the marks of their love on me. Uncle Tony in particular likes leaving bruises behind, showing the world I'm owned.

Nonno grabs my head to hold it still from their pounding as I keep sucking and licking up his shaft, to his balls, and back again. He curses in Italian and I have no idea what it means, but it's so hot it's almost unfair.

This is my safe space, where I'm loved and well and taken care of. Where nothing can hurt me unless I want the pain. I wish I could stay right here forever, surrounded by the men I love and the comfort they bring.

But nothing good lasts forever, and it's Nonno who finishes first.

"Don't swallow," he instructs, and the next thing I know, Uncle Tony kisses me, tasting his father's cum on my tongue as he sucks it. I can't help but moan and my clit throbs. I'm ready to come, but I won't be able to unless one of the guys helps.

My ass stings, and I realize Daddy's slapped it. He does it again, on the other side and harder. He keeps alternating for a minute or two.

"Fuck, you're making her cunt clench," Uncle Tony tells him.

Daddy gives one last echoing slap and pulls his cock out so swiftly, I can feel the burn. He's nearly silent as he comes, covering my reddened ass.

He reaches between Uncle Tony and I, rubbing my clit hard between his fingers.

"Come for us, baby," he says. "Let go. We've got you."

And I do, I come so hard I feel wetness squirting out around Uncle Tony's cock.

"Fuck, tesoro, you feel so good when you do that," Uncle Tony says, and a moment later he practically crushes me to him as he grinds his cock inside me, filling me to the brim.

We stay there, him holding me, Daddy massaging the spots where he slapped, and Nonno stroking my hair.

I'm safe here.

The problem is, they're not.

* * *

As I suspected, all three of them are completely worn out and sleep like babies once dinner is over. I'm exhausted, too, but I have something I need to do first. Quietly, I slink out of the bed we share, and Daddy moves.

I still, one foot in the air, like I'm doing a mannequin challenge.

"Baby?"

"I'm okay. Go back to sleep," I whisper.

He mumbles something unintelligible, and a second later he lets out a small snore. Smirking a little, despite the heavy feeling in my heart, I exit the room, confident with how big the house is, no one will hear me anymore.

I head to my room, where I rarely sleep but have all my stuff set up, and methodically begin to pack. Due to summer courses, the dorms are still open at school, and while I don't want to be there, especially not with the Chois murdered, it's the only place I have to go.

I glance around the room Uncle Tony so painstakingly set up for me, filled with all my favorite things and fandoms. He even got a gigantic Cooky plush that's more than half my size imported. Cooky sits in the corner of the room, his arched eyebrow looking at me accusingly on his pink bunny face.

"Don't look at me like that," I snap at the plushie. "I have to do this. I *have* to."

A part of me whispers, *No, you don't. Stay and let whatever happens happen. You deserve to be happy too.*

"But I won't be happy if anything happens to them."

I sling my laptop bag over my shoulder and heft my overstuffed duffle in my hands as I make my way downstairs, and outside to my car. I look up at the darkened house and hope they don't hate me too much, and that they see the reality of the situation.

Hopefully, this will all be over soon, and I can come back to them, to my home.

Chapter Eight

Tony

I KNOW WHEN one side of my body is cold that something's wrong. Sasha usually sleeps between me and Gene, with Dad on my other side. Gene prefers to be on the edge of the bed. If Sasha's head isn't buried in my chest, then her ass is against my crotch.

This morning, I feel neither, and that girl sleeps like the dead. She's never once been fully awake and out of bed before us unless she had exams.

Sure enough, once I rub sleep from my eyes, I see she's not there. Gene's arm is stretched out, holding nothing.

I whack his arm and he jolts.

"The fuck was that for?"

"Where's Sasha?" I whisper, not wanting to wake Dad.

"She's not in bed?"

Ah, too late. He's up.

"No," I reply, then ask Gene, "Did she get up already?" The bed is cold, she hasn't been in here for a while.

Gene rubs his eyes and says, "I think she got up in the night. It might've been a dream. I dunno."

I don't know why, but something has my stomach in knots. Even if she had insomnia, she would've woken one of us or all of us. I leap out of bed, nearly falling over with my feet tangled in the covers. I disentagle myself as Gene chuckles.

"This isn't funny." I stalk down the hall to her room, hoping she went to sleep in there for whatever reason and hadn't woken us.

At first glance, it looks like everything is normal. Big ass rabbit in one corner, bookcase in the other, Funko dolls on shelves I made and painted, posters of pretty men I am equally jealous of and attracted to on the walls. Especially the fucker with the eight-pack abs.

But her laptop isn't here. Nor is her mouse or mouse pad.

"Sash!" I call as I head downstairs. Maybe she took it to do some work or something in the living room. But I don't smell any coffee brewed, which she definitely would have made.

She's not here. She's not anywhere in the house. I even check the pool in case she wanted to go for a swim.

"Sasha!" I call, heading back inside.

Where the fuck is she?

It's then I see a piece of paper taped to the coffeemaker and yank it off, recognizing Sasha's handwriting and personal stationery.

"Nonno, Daddy, Uncle Tony,

"I'm sorry if I worried you when you didn't find me this morning, but I knew I couldn't discuss this with my three protective but stubborn as fuck men. Obviously the killer we're looking for is my father, this Tomassi, and I can assume you'll find him in your case files.

"But in the event the police look into me in the meantime, I can't be here. I can't be with you. Because what we all have could ruin us. I don't care about me, but you guys built an empire, and I

will not let my unfortunate parentage tear that all down.

"Please be safe, since he's stalking the company. Don't do anything stupid. For once, cooperate with the police if you find anything, and stay alive. I couldn't manage if something happened to any or all of you.

"God willing, this will end and I can come home. But until then, I'm keeping the men I love safe.

"Also, I won't come into work, either. If that's an issue, Nonno, you can fire me. I don't care, as long as you're safe.

"Yours forever,

"Sasha"

I slam the paper on the counter and exclaim, "Son of a bitch!"

"What the fuck is going on?" Dad calls, coming downstairs in his dressing gown, silver hair askew. Gene is on his heels, still looking half asleep.

"This is going on!" I shove the letter at him and he and Gene read silently, and I watch their faces turn from confusion to hurt and then to anger. Which is about how it went down in my head, too.

"Where would she go?" Gene asks. "Gina's?"

"After yesterday, doubtful," Dad replies. "Her dorm, most likely. But we're not going there."

"What? Are you crazy, Dad? She—"

"Basta!" Dad scolds, shutting me up. "She is an adult, and she made a decision. It's a stupid decision, but she made it, and we will not go in like cavemen and drag her back here by the hair."

Honestly, that scenario doesn't sound too bad to me.

"She gave us a task, to find Tomassi's case and turn it over to the police, explain we found him in Collin's old files," Gene says. "This is how we get her back, by making sure no one gets wind of the DNA we tested and getting that motherfucker back behind bars where he belongs."

"Do you remember that name as one of our cases?" I ask, because I don't.

"It would have been Collin's case," Dad reminds me. "Let's get into the office and get back to our search."

"I'll do that," I say. "You two keep up appearances and make excuses as to why Sasha isn't at work." The girl already endeared herself to the other workers, despite whisperings of nepotism. They love her. And why wouldn't they?

It's bad enough what her ex did to her. I'm not letting her have to run or hide anymore. This ends now.

Not typically single-minded, I even skip lunch as I search through all of Collin's old cases. We know it has to be from before he left us, because old Mrs. DiFranco and the Chois are dead. It's not just Collin with whom Tomassi is angry. It's the whole firm.

I vaguely wonder if we should ask the police for escorts, but I also know they'd probably wind up dead before us.

Pausing my search, I page Dad.

"Si?"

"I was wondering if this building and our employees need protection, since DiFranco was killed in the lot and

the Chois were killed after visiting us," I
say.

He curses in a string of Italian so
fast I barely catch it all. "I should have
thought of that. Let me call the Kangs
and get them on it. They have guys, or
they may come themselves."

"Yeah. Maybe get them to send
someone to Sasha's dorm? Just so we
can be sure she's okay? Because Tomassi
may not know she's his kid, but she is
ours, and he wants to take what's ours,"
I say.

"Already on it. I'll have Andrew
get them on the line."

Dad hangs up and I go back to my
search. This guy had to have been put
away sometime after January 2002,
since that's when Sasha was conceived,
so that narrows my search, but we didn't
start automatically digitizing our files

until 2006, so I have 4 years' worth of shit to wade through in paper that Sasha didn't already get to. Thankfully Collin didn't have much more work than I did at the time.

At the bottom of 2003's pile, I see his name.

Andre Tomassi.

And I consulted on this case. Motherfucker...

Now I know why he's out to get us.

* * *

March 2003

Collin and I had a bit of a thing when we were in college, and I was ecstatic he got into Dad's firm with Gene and I. I admit he's not the best lawyer on earth, but it was good to have a familiar face from my time away from this building. He and I never worked together; it was usually Gene.

I was buried up to my eyebrows in paperwork. The problem with being part of the family was that Gene and I had to prove ourselves twice as hard, so that meant more work, harder cases, and a lot of caffeine consumed.

I was working on a file when a knock came at my door.

"Yeah?"

Collin entered, his face looking at once pale and green. "Can we talk?"

Oh shit, he better not want to get back together, I thought. "Sure."

He came in, closed the door, and sat in my visitor's chair. He had a file in his hands. "It's about my case."

I knew he took on the defense in a missing person's and sexual assault case, plus one count of impersonating a police officer. Dad said those were never easy, as we had a job to do, but also a moral obligation to fill.

"Go on."

"This guy, he's vicious, man." Collin slapped the file open, where I could see the bruises left on the two girls he'd been accused of assaulting, and there were details on the internal damage done.

"His friend is going to alibi him out next week, at trial," he continues. "It's an obvious lie, but it will appear solid to the jury. I got told the whole story for closing arguments, but I can't in good conscience let this pass. Not because the friend is lying. I don't give a fuck about that. But this guy should not be out on the streets."

I had to agree, but what was I going to do? "You need to convince the friend not to lie on the stand. Remind him of what he can lose if they figure it out."

"He won't believe me..." Collin trailed off.

"Look, just try. Make sure he knows, say you have to make sure for legal reasons. If he doesn't take the bait ... tell me."

"What are you going to do?" he asked me.

I felt a smile coming to my face. "I'll think of something."

As predicted, the guy didn't back down. But Collin was certain the seed of doubt had been planted. "I just need something to make it grow."

After a quick peek at the file, I got the guy's address. It turned out he wasn't a friend, they had no prior connection. He was a small-time Polish gang member here in Chicago, doing this for the cash.

He seemed a little surprised to find me leaning against his vintage Charger outside his apartment that night.

"Who the fuck are you?" he asked, hands in his pockets.

"Calm down, I'm not here to hurt you. That little peashooter wouldn't even pop off before I beat you to death anyway," I replied, showing him my aluminum baseball bat. "I'm here to make you an offer."

"What kind?"

Ah, the allure of money to those unwilling to make it legally. It was like a moth to a flame.

"If you don't testify, I'll double whatever Tomassi paid you," I tell him.

"And if I tell you no way you have that kinda money and to fuck off?" he countered.

"Then I take away something you love."

He grinned, looking sleazier than I thought possible. "There's not much I love aside from money and my—" He paused, eyes widened at the renewed sight of my bat, now slung over my shoulder.

With practiced ease, I swung the bat and knocked off the side view mirror on his Charger. It hit the sidewalk with a clang.

"What was that now?" I asked, cocking my head. "I'm afraid I didn't hear you." I swung again, this time shattering the driver's side window.

"Stop it!" he demanded, but he also didn't come closer to try and stop me himself. Smart.

"Don't testify, and I will," I replied, casually denting the hood a few times.

"I—"

Passenger's side of the windshield cracked next, echoing in the darkened street. I was grateful no one called the police yet.

"Okay!" he shouted. "Stop it and I won't lie. I'll skip town until he goes to jail. Is that good enough for you to stop torturing my baby?"

I walk over to him and put the bat under his chin, tilting his head up at me.

"I should bash your fucking cogliones off for wanting to let a rapist stay on the streets. But I won't. Just remember, if you testify, I'll be back, and the car won't be the only thing broken when I leave."

* * *

Lo and behold, the next week, the asshole didn't show to testify and Collin gave the most lackluster closing arguments ever. According to the file, Tomassi was sentenced to the max of twenty-five years in prison for aggravated sexual assault and attempted murder.

Looks like he got out early, be it parole or good behavior or time served.

He should have rotted in there.

It was a wild failure for our firm, but one even Dad didn't fault Collin on.

Dad, Gene, and I got together after that and made a rule to never defend sexual assaulters. We worked on an "innocent until proven guilty" belief, but that was one crime none of us could even try to defend in case the client was guilty.

Collin also left the defense side of law after that case. He quit Santini and Sons and went into environmental law, which was where he stayed until he was found dead in the middle of the road by the forest preserve.

I needed to call the jail and see when Tomassi got released, and why, and where he might be now. Getting his parole officer's information was easy enough, as well as finding out he was released three months before Collin was murdered. Which means he was probably planning and researching where Collin was and how to get to us all, one by one. Including DiFranco, who had worked here then.

But what was the Chois' purpose? Just to fuck with us because he saw them come here? Or had he actually been watching us at the club and waited to do something?

The thought of being followed *again* pisses me off and creeps me out. Unless I approve it, I don't like voyeurism.

I make an appointment with Tomassi's parole officer and head to my car, noticing a tall, slim man walking with me. He has on a bucket hat and face mask, but I'd know one of the Kang siblings anywhere. They work fast.

Kang must follow me to the parole officer's office, but I can't spy anybody. Good. That means no one else is aware either.

Or Tomassi already killed him. One or the other.

The parole officer is about my age, but definitely didn't hold up as well as me with his paunchy belly and matching eyebags. He looks like he chose the wrong profession, as most of them do, honestly.

"Mr. Santini, have a seat. Why are you interested in my criminal?" Officer Jones asks.

"Well, my family's firm represented him, and it didn't go well. I'd like to merely get updated on him, so I can update our files," I reply. "I just need his contact info and a recent picture of him."

Am I allowed to ask for that? I don't know. We don't deal often with parole officers. And I don't think he has any idea what he's allowed to give either, because he merely taps on his computer and the printer begins groaning and wheezing. The thing sounds like it needs to go to the grave.

Jones hands me a piece of paper with an address and phone number, both of which I am going to assume are faked, and a photo.

It's the photo that catches my attention.

Because I know that face, and it's not because it shares the same nose with the woman I love.

I saw that face.

Today.

Chapter Nine

Sasha

I MISS THEM.

It's been twelve hours and my heart aches like someone punched it and put it back into my chest. I know they were furious when they found the note. I know Daddy or Uncle Tony went to try and find me or call. And I know Nonno told them to shut up and do their jobs.

It doesn't help that the dorm feels so empty without the Chois here. It would be one thing if they were just away for the summer, but they're not. They're dead, and my father killed them. What he did before he killed them I'd rather not think about.

I want him dead. I want him more dead than Trevor, and considering I plucked Trevor's eyeball out and then bashed his face in with a rock until it was a pile of hamburger meat, that's saying a lot.

I also know I won't get away with murder twice, so I have to hope my men and the cops do their jobs.

If I'm right, my father has no idea who I am, even if he did kill the Chois. He had no idea who my mom was and probably wouldn't know her now if he saw her. So I'm only in danger because of what he can see and know — that I work at Santini and Sons.

My mind wanders to my half-siblings, and I worry if he'll go after them to get back at Daddy, but I don't think so. Mae and Collin worked at

Santini and Sons when he was put away, that's why they're dead.

Why are the Chois dead? Could it be a crime of passion after seeing them at the club, that is, if he followed us there? I mean, Daniel was pretty feminine. And Collin was sodomized with a tree branch.

Ouch. That hurts just to think about.

And another thing, all the murders took place in the daytime or early morning hours. Like, during rush hour. That's an odd pattern and I note it down in my phone. I may have to call one of the guys and at least give them that tidbit.

My stomach growls and I realize I didn't bring food. It's not too late, there's a burger place near the dorm that should still be open, and it's mostly

crowded streets and bright lights.
Nowhere for someone to jump out and
kill me unless I accidentally get caught
in a drive-by.

Decision made, I grab my purse
and head outside into the warm summer
night. As I walk, I remember that Allie,
the other intern, lives nearby, and she's
been asking me to hang out. Usually, I'm
too busy with my men.

*"Hey, it's Sasha. Random, but
wanna grab food near the university?"*
I text. I wait under a shop's awning for a
response when I hear a bloodcurdling
scream down the well-lit alley.

"Help!"

Oh shit. Why did that sound like
Allie of all people? And then a phone
pings, echoing down the gangway. That
must be my text coming through.

Why do these things happen around me?

I dial 9-1-1 when another scream cuts through the night. No one is walking, everyone seems to be behind the wheel tonight. What am I supposed to do?

The operator picks up, "What's your emergency?"

"Fuck," I curse. "Someone's screaming for help down the gangway on the side of the Clark Street Market. It—"

Another scream, this one more desperate than terrified.

"Fucking hurry!" I yell into the receiver and reach into my purse for my pocket knife. I'm not a wannabe hero, but I can't sit here and listen to someone get hurt either. With any luck, it will be some scared teenager who will see someone going to gang up on them and run away.

If only.

Not far down the gangway I enter the alley behind the shops, and yep, there's Allie, all five-foot-nothing of her, laying on the ground, feebly trying to push a man off of her who is at least a foot taller. Her arms don't seem to have any strength in them, and it's no wonder, considering the front of her shirt is slowly soaking in her blood.

It can't be a coincidence, right? That another member of the firm is being attacked? It has to be him.

My father, the serial killer.

He stands up and kicks her in the stomach. I can hear the gasp as the air leaves her lungs. When he starts to undo his belt, that's when I snap out of my stupor.

No you fucking don't.

He's so absorbed in what he's doing, he has no idea I'm coming up behind him.

It's not until my knife is plunged into the meaty part of his upper arm that he knows I'm here. He practically yowls like a wounded cat and jerks away so fast he takes my knife with him, still embedded in his arm.

He turns, and that's when I see his face.

"*Andrew*?"

Nonno's secretary? That's not possible...

And yet it makes perfect sense as to how he knew the Chois were visiting, and when to ambush Mrs. DiFranco, and how he could follow us to the club...

Shit. He must know at least that I'm dating the men, hence why he made snide comments about them being my stepfamily. Did he see Mom when she came yesterday? Does he know who I am to him?

"You little bitch," he growls at me. In the distance, sirens sound, and he makes the decision to run away rather than try and get some revenge. And I have a choice: follow him, or try and help Allie, who is gasping for breath on the ground.

In the end, kindness wins over vengeance, and I bend down, seeing a knife still embedded in her stomach, but she'd been slashed wide open. The knife isn't holding much blood in.

I put my purse down and take my jacket off and press it to the gaping wound.

"Allie, if you can hear me, hold on, okay? Help is coming."

She gurgles and hacks, blood spewing from her mouth. Her wide eyes grow wider still in fear or shock or perhaps both, and then all life goes out in them and her trembling body stills beneath my bloodstained hands.

"No, dammit," I mutter, tears springing to my eyes. "No, not you too."

"Police!" a sharp voice calls. "Step away from the body and put your hands up!"

"Wait, no," I say, standing and going to turn towards the cops. "I'm not—"

A body slams me into the dumpster and before I know it, I'm in handcuffs.

"Don't fucking move," a female officer barks. "You're under arrest."

* * *

141

One good thing about your stepfamily-slash-boyfriends being lawyers, it's easy to have them on retainer.

The moment I got into the station and was put into an interrogation room, I shut up except to ask for my lawyer. I'm not stupid.

However, if they found that DNA match, I may be totally fucked. Who's going to believe me that my ex-step-grandfather's secretary raped my mom twenty years ago and is my biological dad, and accidentally framed me for murders he committed?

I wouldn't believe me.

I can barely hear some sort of commotion outside the interrogation room when the door opens just a sliver.

"—three of you?"

"We're her team, we work together," Daddy snaps as the door opens fully and Uncle Tony walks as fast as he dares over to me.

Nonno and Daddy follow on his heels, shutting the door behind them.

"What on Earth happened? Are you all right? The blood isn't..." Daddy trails off.

"It's not mine," I say, looking down. They didn't even let me wash my hands, which are cuffed in front of me. I'm covered in Allie's dried blood. I swallow hard; now that the guys are here, and I feel a bit of their protective natures, I want to break down after watching someone die like that, but I can't.

"It's Allie's. Our intern."

The room goes dead silent for a moment. Nonno breaks it, but his face is too pale. "Tell us everything that happened."

I do, as calm as possible, starting with me just wanting some food and ending with stabbing the guy in the arm.

"That's when he turned around. I— He—" I take a ragged breath, hating myself for getting emotional, but what human wouldn't?

"It's okay," Daddy says quietly. "Take a breath, it's okay."

"It's Andrew, Nonno," I blurt out. "He's my father, he's been hiding in plain sight, waiting to pick everybody off one by one."

It's then Uncle Tony says something that shocks the shit out of me.

"I know."

"What?" Daddy says, turning towards him.

"That's where I was on my way back from when you called me," he continues. "I found the right case going by dates, went to the parole officer's office, and got the info. I was on my way to tell you both when I was told I needed to come here."

Daddy leans back against the wall when the door bursts open and the two cops who arrested me, along with a plainclothes detective, enter.

"Time for consultation is up. We need to know everything, or we're booking her for the murder," the detective practically snarls.

"Oh, vai a farti fottere," Nonno snaps. "You'll leave our client alone and take the information we have to give you. And I want those handcuffs off of her immediately."

The detective gestures to the female cop, who comes and undoes the cuffs. I want to rub my wrists, but when I try, dried blood flakes onto my jeans.

The cops listen to my story, and then to Uncle Tony's story, although he leaves out that Andrew — Andre — is my father. He ends it with, "He could have more victims out there we didn't know about from before, too. But if you run the DNA against what was in the system from his case, you'll find a match. And he needs to be caught immediately, before more innocent people die."

"Of course," the detective says. "But she was a firsthand witness, so she needs to stay within the state borders until the case is cleared up."

My stomach sinks, thinking we really will have to cancel our trip. No way will these incompetent nitwits find

him in a month. There's going to be a
trail of bodies across Chicagoland; I can
only hope none of them will be ours.

Finally, I am free to go, though no
one apologizes for how they treated me.
Daddy walks with his arm around my
shoulders until he helps me in the
backseat of Nonno's car. Uncle Tony
gets in on my other side and I finally let
the tears flow.

Not only the carnage I witnessed,
but the fact that *that* was how I met my
father after all these years broke
something in me.

Reality was sinking in, and I
didn't like it. I didn't want it.

Every little kid wants to believe
the best of their parents, and for Mom,
though we haven't gotten along the
whole time, I did have the best. For my
father, I was able to imagine anything I

wanted, to dream he was this amazing person. The dream was shattered tonight.

Daddy holds me to his chest, and Uncle Tony rubs my back as Nonno drives to my dorm.

"I'm going to get her things. We can pick up her car another time," he says, getting out of the car. He takes a bag and I realize it's my stuff the police confiscated. It has my student ID which gets me into the dorm building.

I hadn't even thought to ask for any of my stuff.

Nor do I argue that they are taking me back home. With them is the only place I ever want to be.

"I wish I could have saved her," I whisper against Daddy's chest.

"Nothing could have saved her if she lost that much blood, baby," he says.

"You made sure she wasn't alone in the end. You did what you could."

If that was the best I could do, it felt pathetic. "Hi, this person is dying. Sit there with them and do absolutely nothing else to save them because it's impossible." It's not enough, and I can't explain that to them. I can barely explain it to myself. Saying that being with them is enough feels like a cop-out, a way to make the living feel better.

Nonno comes back, puts my bags in the trunk, and drives us home in silence.

Once we're inside the house, Uncle Tony prods me upstairs. "Go shower. I will toss your clothes."

"And buy you new shoes tomorrow," Daddy adds.

My favorite Converse platforms
are now good for nothing except a
horror movie or the trash. Tragic.

I do as commanded, wanting
nothing more than to get clean, knowing
I'll still see my blood-encrusted hands in
my mind's eye for the rest of my life.

When I get out of the shower and
dry off and get in my bathrobe, the guys
are all waiting for me in the master
bedroom. I slip off my bathrobe and let
it fall to the floor, needing comfort.
Needing to forget.

Nonno takes my hand and pulls
me to him, kissing me breathless before
pushing me back onto the bed. Uncle
Tony leans over and kisses my lips and
neck, while Daddy and Nonno take turns
on my breasts, moving lower down my
stomach, skirting my core, down to my
thighs.

"Open up, tesoro," Uncle Tony whispers, and I do, his half-hard cock slipping past my lips as I close my eyes. "Good girl. This is what you were meant for, pleasure, not pain."

"Or both," Daddy suggests, and Uncle Tony chuckles.

I look over to see Nonno removing his boxers, stroking himself and Daddy at the same time. It makes me moan, which in turn sends vibrations up Uncle Tony's cock.

"Fuck, do that again," he says, hand gripping my hair tight.

I do, and feel his cock twitch on my tongue.

Just as I do that, Nonno slips inside me. I'm already perfectly wet and I spread my legs wider as I feel Daddy come close.

"Hold still up there," he tells
Uncle Tony, and he lifts me, turning me
to the side. Uncle Tony turns my head
until I'm comfortable, and now his cock
hits the back of my throat.

I take him deeper as I feel
another cock stretching my pussy and
my whole body tenses up.

"Shhh," Daddy says. "Loosen up,
baby. Let Daddy fuck you. You know you
want both our cocks, don't be scared."
He starts to caress my clit, turning me
on even more as his long cock slides
fully inside me.

It hurts, but the pain nearly
blanks my mind as he and Nonno begin
moving in tandem.

"Our beautiful little whore,"
Nonno says sweetly. "We won't let
anything bad happen to you. You're

ours, you belong to us, and nothing will take you from us. Ever."

"No one could take cock so well," Uncle Tony adds. "You were made just for this."

I whimper and he thrusts deeper into my throat. I do my best to swallow around him, but he's so thick.

"This; this is exactly how everything is meant to be," Daddy adds.

I try to move my eyes to look at him and catch him and Nonno as Nonno sticks his tongue down his throat and it's so hot I want to combust.

This was exactly what I needed. To shut my mind down and let my body feel everything instead of my heart. I close my eyes, focusing on the pressure and heaviness of Uncle Tony in my mouth, and the friction and burn of the two cocks pounding inside me.

This really was what I was made for.

I whine as I feel myself reaching climax, but unable to get there.

Uncle Tony chuckles. "This is the only suffering you'll get, tesoro. You come when we say you can, not before." He holds my head and I feel him spasm before cum coats the back of my throat. I swallow and choke as he keeps coming, then finally pulls out as I gasp for breath.

He moves down my body, nipping my breasts and squeezing my ass as he makes his way down as well.

I prop myself on my elbow and watch as he licks both cocks as they enter and exit my pussy, dizzy from how erotic he looks, how I know it's wrong but fuck, makes me feel so right.

"I think our little one enjoyed enough of the show," Nonno comments.

Uncle Tony nods and moves to lick around my throbbing clit. He reaches his hand around and I feel his fingers penetrate my ass dry. I try to squirm, but he's holding me still and the others are still fucking me like machines.

Finally, it's all too much and the second Uncle Tony sucks my clit between his lips, I climax. I feel Nonno come inside me first, and then Daddy, who pulls out and sprays the last of it on my hip and thigh.

My whole body trembles, but I'm too weak to move.

Nonno rolls me onto my back and Uncle Tony grabs my thighs, keeping them open as he licks me clean, bringing me to the edge of another orgasm but not letting me go over.

"That's a promise for tomorrow," he whispers to me.

In the dark, under the covers, surrounded by the men who love me, I think everything just might be okay.

Chapter Ten

Sasha

NEEDLESS TO SAY, I didn't sleep well that night, and it's been a week and I am still not quite right.

The guys are working remotely, which Nonno didn't want to do until I sat in his lap and pouted. That won him over.

"You realize we're totally screwed if she can make us do what she wants just by looking cute, right?" Uncle Tony said to Nonno.

"Oh, kid, we were screwed the moment she turned eighteen; she doesn't even have to try," Nonno replied.

I also discovered we were being watched, but not by the bad guys. My men knew the leaders of an international, um, organization who offered protection for a fee. They'd used them before, apparently, and were doing so again now on us and the whole Santini and Sons building.

"It's easy for Andrew — Andre, to know where we live," Daddy says. "He had access to most of our personnel files. So we have to be careful."

"And that means he knew exactly who I was the whole time," I add, shivering. "He'd only worked for us for three months, but he could even have Mom's address."

"Which is why she and my grandchildren are under the protection of the leader. He won't let anything get past him. Two of them and their employees are at the building, and the final lead member is here with us," Nonno explains.

That actually makes me feel even worse. I feel like I should be doing something as I type up a report on the case so far. Here were the bulletpoints I had.

-Collin Gross caught the rape and murder case.

-Collin begged Uncle Tony to help because he didn't want Andre to get off on a lesser charge, or cleared completely.

-Uncle Tony made the guy who was going to testify and lie run off.

-Andre got put away for nineteen years.

-Got out immediately plotting revenge, got a fake identity, and applied

to be Nonno's secretary, with us none
the wiser.

And now he had killed five people
with more on his list. And nobody has
any fucking clue where he is or how to
find him. The addresses he gave Nonno
and the parole officer were both fake.
His number was disconnected.

He is a ghost, or rather demon,
skulking about, waiting to kill again.

Nonno, Daddy, and Uncle Tony
have to go into their respective rooms to
do a remote staff meeting with the other
attorneys, which they do monthly, so I'm
on my own in the living room
downstairs, trying not to stay worried
but at the same time unable to stop
myself from worrying.

I try to watch TV to distract
myself when my phone pings twice. I
check and it's a number I don't have

saved. Rolling my eyes, I go to delete it, when I see the preview of the media attached.

It's a picture of my mom's house.

Hands trembling, I open the message and read what's been typed:

"Come meet me where I killed that cute little intern, or the next one will be Maggie. And if you call the police or tell your men, your mother will wish I'd killed her back when we made you."

Bile rises in my throat and I sway, dizzy with the sudden rush of fear in my veins. That fucking sick bastard. What could he want with me besides killing me? Yet, somehow, that message didn't sound like he wanted me there to hurt me. Maybe he had a message for my men? But that also makes no sense. He could just as easily contact them.

I want to tell him to fuck off, but I know how vicious he is, and I know he'll hurt my sister if I don't give in. Her life, my entire family's lives, are more important to me than my own. This is my father; technically, he is my responsibility. Anything he did that I could have stopped and didn't would be my responsibility.

I have to go.

I leave a note for the guys saying I went for a drive to clear my head. None of them need to know and rush over, possibly getting one of them killed in the process. I do, however, turn my phone's location on. It's how they found me before when my ex kidnapped me, so it could come in handy again.

Parking on the street as close to that alley as I can, I pay the meter and steel myself for this confrontation. I don't know what to expect, or what to say or do. I just know I have to be here. A thought of calling the police now runs through my mind, but if he hears me somehow, then what?

I turn on my phone's voice recorder just in case and slip it into my pocket as I begin to walk down the alley. The place where Allie's body was is roped off, and standing in front of it is him.

Andre.

My father.

This is so fucked up.

"Sasha," he says, his voice no longer as lilting and fake friendly as it was when he pretended to be Nonno's secretary.

"Tomassi," I reply.

He spreads his hands. "No 'Dad'? Or is that just what you call one of the men you fuck?"

My face heats, but I don't take the bait. That's what he wants, and I won't give it to him. "You asked me to be here. What do you want?"

"Can't a man want to officially meet his daughter?"

"Your unfortunate sperm made me, but you are *not* my father," I reply.

He smirks. He really does look like me, especially the nose and chin. Fuck, a part of me wants plastic surgery now.

"Sasha, I wanted to tell you who I was the moment I spoke to Gene and discovered your little slut of a mother," he says.

"Don't," I say through clenched teeth. "Don't you dare speak of her after what you did!"

He shrugs. "I'd rather talk about you anyway."

"What about me?" This is not how I expected this to go, but then again, I didn't expect much anyway. Still, this is weird.

"I killed the other women I chose, didn't you read that in my file?" he asks.

I nod.

"Yet your mother lived. And you, with your brilliant mind, never wondered why?"

He had me there. I never once thought of it. Not even to hypothesize. "Well, I'm wondering now."

He steps closer, and I can smell cheap cologne and sweat and feel sick. It's broad daylight, but there's no one

around with it being a Monday.
Nowhere I can go to escape unless he
lets me. I have to see this through.

"Your mother lived for one reason
and one reason only — you."

"Me?"

"I admit I hoped for a boy, but
with the way you behave, I don't think it
matters all that much," he says, smiling.

"You let my mom live because
you wanted her to get pregnant," I say
slowly, realization dawning. But ... why?
"You wanted a kid."

"I wanted an heir, someone to
join me, to partake of life the way I do:
forcefully, vigorously, taking what we
want without permission or obedience."

This guy is totally fucking screwy.

"And you want me to join you and
be what? Robin to your Rapeman?"

He laughs. The nutty fuck actually laughs!

"Amusing. I admit I don't quite have your sense of humor, but I do enjoy it." He moves closer and I force myself not to flinch. He doesn't hurt me, just pushes my hair away from my shoulder. "You do look like your mother, too. She was beautiful, I imagine still is. But you have that little bit of darkness from me. How else could you fuck your stepfamily while they also fuck each other, hm? There has to be something just a bit off about you. And that's what you got from me."

"I got *nothing* from you," I hiss.

"Really? You think how you and they behave is normal, good behavior? No, my dear, it's not. However, I can see the appeal." His eyes linger down my body and bile creeps up my throat.

"I still don't understand why you asked me here," I say to distract him. "Because you want to convince me to be your ... partner?"

He nods. "Precisely. It was always my goal, in addition to punishing those who wrongfully put me away. How delighted I was to find you so close!"

"Sorry to disappoint you, but I want absolutely nothing to do with you," I tell him. I try to step back when he grabs my wrist so tight I'm afraid a bone might snap. Controlling my breathing becomes a chore, and I want to have a panic attack but can't. I need to be clear-headed to get out of this alive and unscathed.

It's then I see someone enter the alley and I both fear for them and am grateful. Will he kill them if he sees them? Will he kill us both? Or will he run away? I pray for the third option.

I try to keep my eyes on him as the figure gets closer and I see … it's a woman. Maybe my height, long dark hair, sunglasses, and big stomper boots. She's older than me, maybe twenty-five? And she's walking like she knows exactly what she stumbled onto.

"You're not leaving here, Sasha. You're coming with me one way or another. I prefer it to be willing, but we all know that's not a dealbreaker for me," Andre says, yanking me as close as possible.

It's easier for me to look past him now, and the woman has … is that a knife? If she tries to play hero, she could get us both killed, but definitely her. I wish I had a way to warn her to leave, but I can't.

For the recording, I say, "You're saying you'll what? Take me and rape me? And then what? Kill me?"

He laughs. "Oh no, Sasha. I'll keep doing it until I either break you, or you agree to stay with me and have the same sort of freedom I do."

"Madness is not freedom," I reply, wishing I could vanish right now. The mental images he put in my head make me feel sick.

The woman is close now, somehow silent in those boots. Whatever is going to happen will happen any minute now, and I'm terrified of the outcome.

What I need to do is distract Andre, so I loosen my tense stance.

"If I come with you, no more killing people I know."

He arches his eyebrow. "You're willing to give yourself up to save others? That you definitely didn't get from me."

"Those are my terms. I will even do my best to get the guys not to look for you anymore."

I lie so easily, that is something I am glad I got from him.

His grin is so slimy I feel like someone put slugs on my body as I watch it form on his face. His other arm goes around my waist and I'm ready to go into fight or flight mode when he suddenly stills, then stiffens, a ragged, breathy groan coming from his lips.

He gets heavier, and I leap back, no longer in a viselike grip, and watch his body tumble to the floor. He's alive, but unmoving, and then I see why.

The knife embedded at the base of his spine paralyzed him.

I look up and meet the girl's warm brown eyes.

"I don't know how you did that, but thank you," I gasp out. My legs are weak from adrenaline and relief, and she immediately comes around and grabs me, steadying me.

She smiles, as if she didn't just stab a man. "I'm Julie. Julie Kang. Mr. Santini hired my guys and I to protect everyone at the firm. I've been tailing you for days, keeping you safe."

And I didn't notice? That's ... not good. I thought she was only at the house.

"I informed your men, they'll be here soon with the police," she continues. "Amazing and brave of you to distract him for me. I thank you. You definitely saved your life, and made me not have to fight anybody." She grins at me. "Not that I don't enjoy a good fistfight now and again."

I go to speak when I see three distinct shadows in the distance. Already recognizing them, I break away from her and into my men's embrace, letting the tears flow. Only now do I realize how terrified I actually was, and how close I came to a fate worse than death.

But they protected me, even if it wasn't them physically.

"It's over, tesoro," Uncle Tony whispers. "It's finally over."

Epilogue

Sasha

SEOUL IS BEAUTIFUL, even if this trip is bittersweet. This was the vacation I needed, and the guys and I even took a 2 day trip to Jeju Island. Have you ever had sex under the moonlight, on the rocks by the beach? We found a long, flat one, and well, I want to do it again. Like, immediately.

But tonight is our last full day and night in Seoul, and Nonno, Daddy, and Uncle Tony said they have a surprise for me and I should bring a jacket.

I wear my red dress, the one I wore to the club, and a black silk bomber jacket I bought here in Seoul on top of it. We take a car to the center of Seoul, to Namsan Tower. We went here already, so I'm a little confused as to why we're back.

"There's something we didn't do last time that we were saving for tonight," Daddy tells me as Nonno helps me out of the car.

"But the tower is closed to visitors now," I remind him.

"Not for everyone."

I jump at the unexpected voice and see the girl who had stopped my father that night standing there with three men, two of whom were definitely related to each other, if not all three.

"Julie Kang, right?" I say.

She nods. "These are my husbands, Eun-si, Jeong-won, and Seo-ji."

Oh shit, I guess I'm not the only one around here with multiple men. I want to ask her how she managed to marry them all, but I figure now is not the time.

"We'll let you in, just let us know when you're coming out so we know it's you," the man named Seo-ji says. He's tall and broad, with coiffed, dyed-blond hair. He walks over and places something in Uncle Tony's hand, but I can't see what it is before he slips it into his pocket.

"Gamsahapnida," I say.

"Not bad. Your accent needs work," he replies as one of the other men, Eun-si I think, holds the door open for us.

Daddy holds me by the waist as we take an elevator and head to the observation deck. I know what's up here but...

"I thought they were forced to take these all down!" I exclaim as we exit onto the deck, where the Love Padlocks run along its length, thousands of metal and plastic locks inscribed with names and initials of lovers come before us.

"Paris and New York did. Not here," Nonno says.

Uncle Tony takes a red heart lock out of his pocket. So that's what Seo-ji gave him.

Daddy hands me a permanent marker. "Write whatever you want on it, baby. Then we'll lock it up and throw away the key, so it can't ever be undone."

I take the lock and write a large S, and around it our first initials. The Santinis, forever and always. Finding a

spot on the railing, Uncle Tony helps me
fix it and I put our birth months as the
combination.

He then hands me the key.
Risking any germs that may be on it, I
kiss the key before throwing it with all
my might into the greenery below.
Everything had tried to undo our love.
Nothing would undo this. Ever.

It's so beautiful up here at night, I
take a moment to stare out at the lights
and mountains. I've been through so
much, so damn much, and I only made
it thanks to these three men. I can never
begin to explain what they mean to me.

"Sasha?"

I turn towards Uncle Tony's voice
and am thankful for that railing, or else
I'd probably have fallen over.

He's kneeling. He has a ring.

Oh shit, are they going to make me choose?

"No," I blurt.

"We haven't asked you anything yet," Nonno comments.

"We?" I turn towards him and Daddy, confused.

Daddy nods. "Aside from having connections to get us up here privately, there's a reason we wanted to ensure you saw and met all four of the Kangs."

"Julie fell in love with the brothers against her better judgment, much like you did with us," Uncle Tony continues. "And the brothers are much like the three of us as well."

"She said she married them all," I comment.

Nonno nods. "Legally, on paper, she married Eun-si, the youngest, as the oldest is technically not allowed to marry foreigners. But they had a ceremony for all four of them."

"I've never been married," Uncle Tony says. "And to marry the man who once married your mom might be weird, so the three of us decided I'd be the one to marry you on paper, which is why I'm the one holding the ring."

I feel my heart melting, but this isn't a fairytale, and I need to remind them of that before I go and do something stupid like agree.

"But, still, we were family. What if—"

"Tesoro." Uncle Tony's voice is firm. "Whatever comes our way, we can fight it. Our love is worth fighting for."

"What if you lose everything because of me?" I ask, hating how small my voice sounds.

Daddy comes behind me and wraps his arms around me. "Baby, whatever happens, we'll survive as long as we're together. Nothing we're doing is illegal, and if anyone takes away the business, we'll still be okay. What matters is having you with us as long as you want to be."

I practically melt into him as I turn back to Uncle Tony. "What about kids?"

"If you want them one day, I'm game. Again, I don't have any, I'm the logical choice," he replies. "And if you don't want them, or you want to adopt, whatever. We're here for it."

"We are here for it all, cara mio," Nonno clarifies.

"So, Sasha? What do you say?" Uncle Tony asks. "Will you marry us,

will you be ours for the rest of our
lives?"

I almost say no again; my fear of
them losing everything because they
love me is so prevalent. But I've nearly
died multiple times now. What's life if I
don't live it?

"Yes, I'll marry you. All of you.
Just please never let me go."

Uncle Tony slips a ring on my
finger — a teardrop shaped diamond
surrounded by a ruby and an emerald
like the Italian flag on either side — and
gets up off the ground.

In turn, each one of them kisses
me; I move from man to man faster than
I can conceive, ending up back in
Daddy's arms.

They cuddle me close, enclosing
me in their warmth as a cool breeze
whips past us.

We've made it through
kidnappings, divorces, secrets, even a
near prison sentence.

Nothing, ever, can tear us apart.

The End

About the author

S.L. Sinclair is a dark romance and taboo author fascinated with human sexuality, murder, and psychology. *Beyond Her Duties* was her first release, which made her an international bestseller. Followed by the surprise smash hit *The Family Firm*, cementing her in the dark and taboo genres of romance.

They're part of the LGBT+ community as bisexual and nonbinary and uses she/they pronouns.

When not writing, she's watching horror movies and has her nose buried in whatever book is closest. Sometimes

she actually goes outside.

You can find them on Facebook,

Twitter, Goodreads, BookBub, and

Instagram.